This Ladybird book
belongs to

. . . .

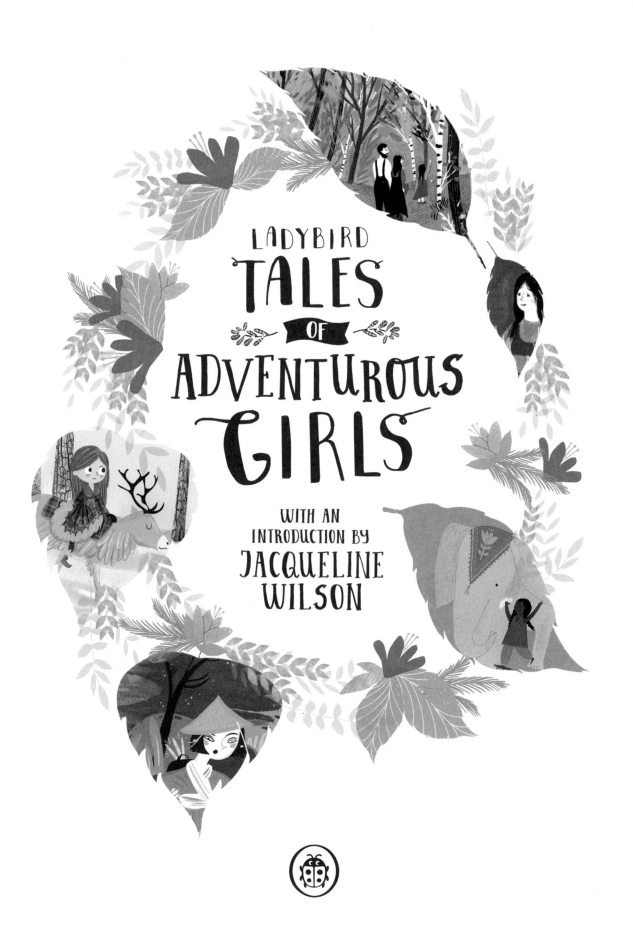

LADYBIRD
TALES
OF
ADVENTUROUS
GIRLS

WITH AN
INTRODUCTION BY
JACQUELINE
WILSON

CONTENTS

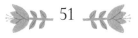

INTRODUCTION

When I was a little girl I loved reading fairy stories, especially if they were about beautiful princesses with long curly hair who wore frilly dresses down to their satin slippers. (I was a plain child with short straight hair, my dresses didn't have a single frill and my mother made me wear ugly sensible shoes.) But after a while I got a bit tired of all these princesses. They seemed a rather silly bunch, for all their beauty. They let themselves be outwitted by bad fairies and wicked stepmothers, and were rendered helpless by pricking their fingers or eating poisoned apples. They then fell into a deep sleep and languished for years until a handsome prince just happened to come along and rescue them.

Why couldn't they rescue themselves? I wanted them to outwit the baddies in the books. It would be wonderful if they were clever and courageous and prepared to go on amazing adventures. I'd have loved to read the six stories about adventurous girls in this fantastic book. None of the heroines happen to have long curly hair or frilly frocks or satin slippers. All of them are brave and resourceful, and they face up to terrifying dangers and disasters. They might get just as scared as you or me if *we* were captured by a wicked witch or a blue troll or a sea serpent – but they work out ways to get the better of them.

I don't know whether any of these girls ever went to school, but they certainly get top marks for being imaginative and quick-witted and daring. They know how to cure sick elephants and be royally rewarded, they work out how to water crops during a terrible drought, and, if their dearest friend disappears, they set out on a terrifying journey and rescue him!

All power to Gretel and Tamasha and Tokoyo and Chandra and Sea Girl and Gerda! They come from different countries and traditions but they're all such marvellous spirited girls I wish each one could be my best friend. When you've read each of their stories perhaps you'd like to pretend they'll all meet up together and talk of their adventures and laugh and sing and dance far into the night.

Jacqueline Wilson

Jacqueline Wilson

GRETEL
AND
HANSEL

A tale from the Brothers Grimm

Illustrated by

OLGA BAUMERT

retel and her older brother, Hansel, lived with their father, a poor woodcutter, and their stepmother, an unkind woman who didn't like children.

"Winter is coming and we don't have enough food," the stepmother said to her husband one night, when Gretel and Hansel were in bed. "Those children of yours eat too much. We must take them into the forest and leave them there."

"We can't do that!" said the children's father.

"Don't be a fool," their stepmother said. "If we don't, we will *all* starve."

Upstairs, too hungry to sleep, Gretel listened to every word. She woke Hansel and told him what she'd heard.

"If they leave us in the forest," Gretel said, "we must try to find our way home again."

Hansel had an idea that he whispered to his sister. Gretel nodded.

As soon as their father and stepmother were asleep, Hansel crept out of the house and filled his pockets with smooth white pebbles. Then he went back to bed.

The next day, Gretel and Hansel's stepmother led them out of the house.

"We are all going into the forest to chop wood," she said.

Gretel ran ahead to distract her father and stepmother. She asked all sorts of questions about the animals and plants in the forest while Hansel walked behind, dropping pebbles on the ground as he went.

Eventually, they all stopped in a clearing and the children's father made a fire.

"Wait here and keep warm while your stepmother and I go and chop wood," he said sadly, and he gave his children a big hug.

Gretel and Hansel nodded, but they knew their father and stepmother would not return.

They waited until dark, then they followed Hansel's trail of white stones, which gleamed in the moonlight, all the way back home.

The woodcutter was overjoyed to see his children, but his wife was very angry.

"Get to bed!" she shouted, and slammed the door behind them.

It wasn't long before Gretel and Hansel's stepmother again started plotting to get rid of them.

"We'll have to take them deeper into the wood tomorrow," she told their father, "so it will be impossible for them to find their way back."

The children overheard their stepmother's wicked plan.

"You need to collect more pebbles," Gretel said to Hansel, determined not to be lost in the woods.

But, when Hansel tried to sneak out like he had before, he found that his stepmother had locked the door.

"Don't worry," said Gretel. "We'll think of something else."

The next day, the children's father gave them some dry old bread to eat. Hansel kept his piece and dropped crumbs from it as they walked through the forest.

They went much further this time. Then, just as before, Gretel and Hansel's father and stepmother left them behind.

When it got dark, the children looked for the trail of breadcrumbs in the moonlight, but the crumbs had gone. The birds had eaten them all!

All night and all the next day, the children wandered through the forest, getting more and more lost and very, very hungry. They were about to give up when a white bird flew down and fluttered ahead of them. It led them to a strange little cottage.

"Look, Gretel!" cried Hansel, running over. "This house is made of gingerbread, and cake and marzipan!"

Both children began nibbling on pieces of the delicious cottage when the front door opened. An old woman came out and peered at them through thick glasses.

"You children look very hungry," she said, smiling kindly. "Come into my house and have some supper."

Inside the gingerbread cottage, the dining table was covered with delicious food and drink such as Gretel and Hansel had only ever dreamed of before.

Once they had eaten and drunk as much as they could, the old woman let them sleep on the most comfortable beds they had ever seen.

"This is wonderful," said Hansel, snuggling down.

Gretel wasn't so sure. How would they ever repay the kind old woman? But, before she could worry too much, she fell into a deep sleep.

Early the next morning, the old woman came in and pulled Hansel from his bed. She was angry.

"You children belong to me now!" she hissed.

"Stop, you witch!" cried Gretel. "You're hurting him!"

The old woman ignored her and locked Hansel in a cage.

"You, girl, must cook for your brother until he is fat enough for me to eat!" she cackled.

So every day Gretel cooked and slaved, and every day the witch – who was half blind – pinched Hansel's finger to see how fat he was getting.

Gretel was a clever girl. One day she waited until the old woman was asleep, then she gave Hansel a chicken bone to poke out of the cage instead of his finger.

"This will fool the witch into thinking you aren't getting any fatter," she whispered.

The old woman would pinch Hansel's finger, but no matter how long she waited it always seemed to stay thin and bony.

Finally, the witch lost patience. "I will eat the boy now anyway!" she shouted at Gretel. "Go and check the oven is hot enough."

Gretel went over to the oven. She didn't know what to do. How could she save her brother from being eaten? Suddenly she had a bright idea. "I don't know how to check the oven," she said slyly. "Can you show me?"

"You stupid child," said the old woman, as she pushed Gretel away and leaned inside the oven.

Quick as a flash, Gretel bundled the witch into the flames and slammed the door. Then she broke open Hansel's cage with a poker. The two children hugged each other tightly.

"Can you reach that pot up on the high shelf, Hansel?" Gretel asked. "I saw the witch put gold and precious stones inside it."

Hansel grabbed the pot. Inside, many jewels, coins and other riches sparkled. "Quick, Gretel! Let's try to find our way back to Father."

The children packed up some food and raced away through the forest. Eventually, they found their way home.

Their father hugged them tightly. "I'm so sorry," he said. "I should never have left you in the forest." Then he told them their nasty stepmother had died.

"We forgive you, Father," the children said.

Hansel told their father all about the gingerbread cottage, and how brave Gretel had saved them both from the scary witch.

Gretel emptied out the pot. "Look, Father," she said, as the jewels and gold coins tumbled on to the table.

Their father couldn't believe his eyes!

Gretel and Hansel were very happy to be home. And, thanks to the witch's treasure, they never went hungry again.

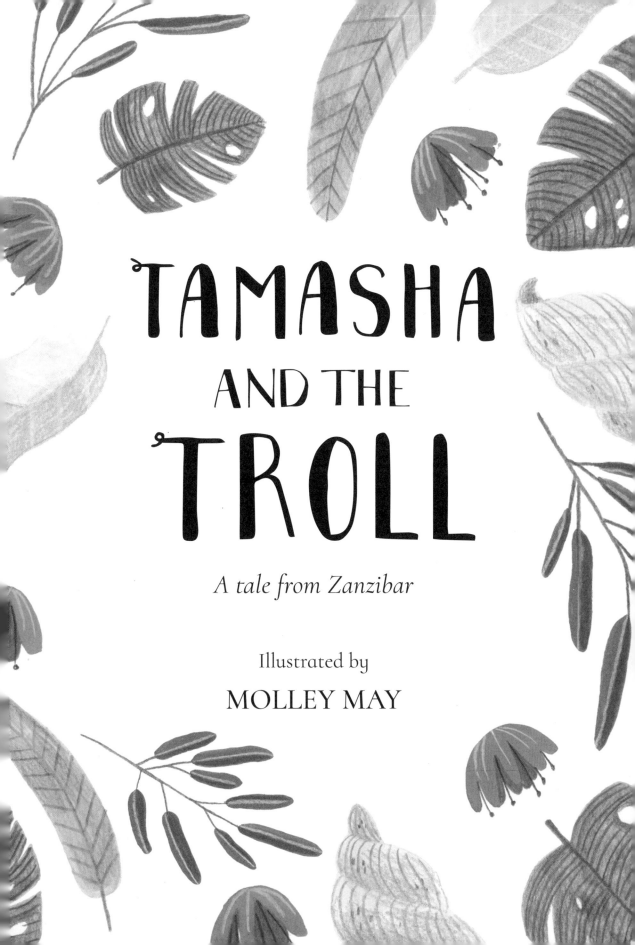

TAMASHA
AND THE
TROLL

A tale from Zanzibar

Illustrated by

MOLLEY MAY

Tamasha lived with her mother and her two older sisters, Tisha and Tosha, in a village on the beautiful island of Zanzibar. One day Tisha and Tosha asked their mother if they could go down to the beach and play.

"Only if you take your little sister with you," their mother said sternly.

"But she will slow us down," grumbled Tosha. "She's always running off to explore and getting lost."

"If she doesn't go, then neither do you," said their mother.

So off the three sisters went, down the long path to the sea.

"Don't you go anywhere without us," Tisha said to Tamasha, as she and Tosha rushed into the waves, laughing and splashing.

Tamasha sighed. *I would much rather be searching for a tree to climb*, she thought. But instead she paddled at the water's edge.

As Tamasha waded into the shallow water, a wave carried a beautiful shell, as white as the moon, on to the beach.

"Oh! How beautiful," said Tamasha. She picked up the shell and put it to her ear. Inside she could hear the soft *swoosh* of the sea. It sounded like music, so she made up a song to sing along with the sea-sound while she waited for her sisters.

When it was time to go home, Tamasha and her sisters started back up the path.

"Oh no! Wait!" cried Tamasha, when they were halfway home. "I forgot my shell! I must go back and get it."

"Well, you'll have to catch us up," said Tisha with a scowl.

"We won't wait," said Tosha, sticking her nose in the air.

But Tamasha wasn't listening – she was already running back to the beach.

"There you are, lovely shell," she said, grabbing it from the rock where she had left it. Then she began to sing her song again.

But hiding behind the rock was a wicked Zimwi troll.

"That's a pretty song, little girl," he said, jumping out in front of Tamasha.

And, before she knew what was happening, the Zimwi grabbed her and pushed her into a big drum he was carrying.

"You can sing for my supper!" he shouted, pulling the drum-skin tight so that Tamasha was trapped inside.

The Zimwi bent over the drum and banged on the skin again and again. "Whenever I beat the drum like this, you must sing!" he commanded. "Understand?"

Tamasha didn't want to sing for the troll. But she knew that she wouldn't be able to escape straight away. So, as he beat the drum, she started to sing, as he had ordered.

"Very good!" said the Zimwi. Then he picked up the drum and off they went.

After a while they came to a village and the Zimwi called out, "Bring me some food and I will play my magical singing drum for you!"

As soon as the villagers had gathered round the fire, the Zimwi started to beat the drum. Tamasha took a deep breath and sang her sweet shell song. The people were amazed and gave the Zimwi as much food as he could eat.

And so each day the Zimwi travelled to a different village, banging his "magical" drum to make Tamasha sing, and every time the villagers gave the greedy Zimwi all the food he could ever wish for.

Sometimes Tamasha changed the words to her song, but the Zimwi didn't seem to notice.

Then, one day, they came to Tamasha's own village.

"Bring me some food," called the Zimwi, "and I will play you my magical drum."

"I will cook you fish and rice," a woman replied, and Tamasha realized at once that it was her mother's voice. She thought quickly. How could she let her mother know she was trapped inside the drum? Then she had an idea.

This time, when the villagers crowded round the fire to hear the Zimwi play, Tamasha changed the words of her song. Now the beautiful tune told the story of a little girl who had found a shell on the beach. When her sisters heard this, they ran to their mother.

"It's Tamasha!" they cried. "We've found her. Tamasha is in the drum!"

Tamasha's mother couldn't believe her ears. They had searched and searched for Tamasha ever since Tisha and Tosha had come home without her. And now quick-witted Tamasha was tricking the Zimwi right under his own nose!

But Tamasha's mother knew she would have to outwit the Zimwi even further to get her daughter back.

Tamasha's mother marched straight up to the Zimwi. "If you will go and get some water from the river for us to have with our meal, I will bring you your food."

Reluctantly, the Zimwi agreed. As soon as he was out of sight, Tamasha's mother tore back the drum-skin and found her little girl inside. She pulled Tamasha out and hugged her tight. Tisha and Tosha cried with happiness to see their sister.

"We must teach this Zimwi a lesson," said Tamasha's mother.

"But how?" asked Tosha.

"I know," said Tamasha. "Take a burning stick from the fire and follow me." She picked up the drum and led her mother and sisters to a rotten tree at the edge of the village.

"Put the burning stick in there," she said.

And, when they did, the smoke drove a swarm of bees out and right into the drum. Tamasha quickly pulled the drum-skin closed, took the drum back to the fireside and climbed up a nearby tree to hide.

When the Zimwi returned with the water, the villagers asked him to play again before they brought out the food. Proudly, he started to beat his drum. But, to his surprise, it did not sing. He banged harder, but still he heard nothing except a strange buzzing sound.

"Sing, drum!" he shouted.

The villagers began to laugh.

The Zimwi threw the drum on the ground and kicked it. But still it wouldn't sing, and the villagers laughed louder.

By now the Zimwi was furious. He picked up the drum and stormed off. "I will make you sing if it is the last thing I do, girl," he snarled, and ripped off the drum-skin.

The bees poured out and surrounded him, stinging him wildly. The Zimwi screamed and ran out of the village, with the cloud of bees swarming after him.

"You can't fool us!" Tamasha shouted from the tree, as the Zimwi raced away and the villagers cheered.

The next day, all the children in the village followed brave Tamasha as she went exploring on the beach. They climbed every tree in sight with her, just to hear over and over about how she had tricked the troll.

And as for the Zimwi – he was never seen again!

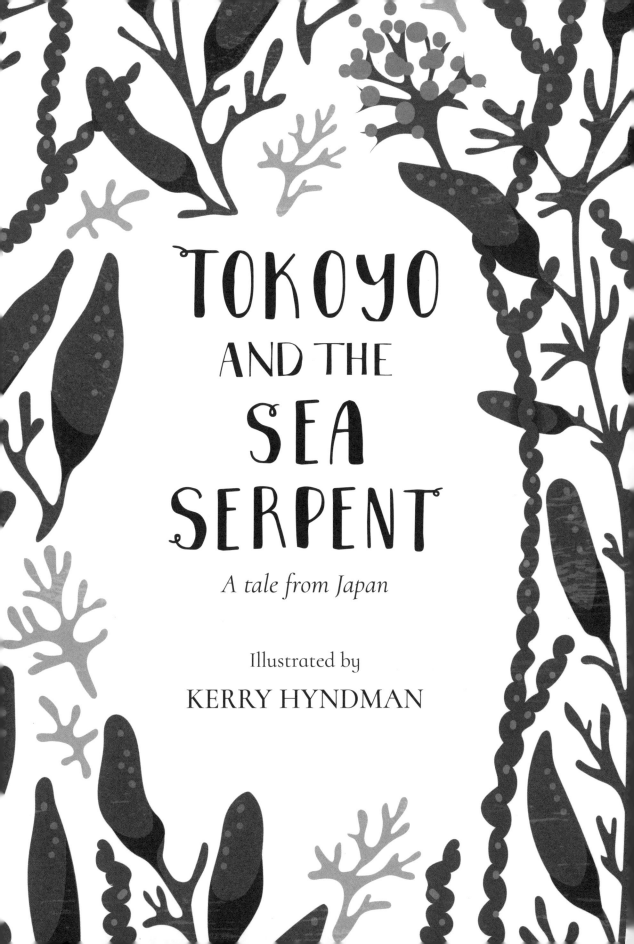

TOKOYO
AND THE
SEA
SERPENT

A tale from Japan

Illustrated by

KERRY HYNDMAN

**A** very long time ago in Japan, there was a young girl called Tokoyo. She lived with her father, Oribe Shime, who was the Emperor's favourite samurai warrior.

Tokoyo's father loved her very much and taught her the ways of the samurai: how to fight with a dagger, shoot with a bow and arrow, ride a horse, and – above all – to protect the weak, and be brave and loyal. Tokoyo dreamed of being a samurai like her father.

When Oribe Shime was away serving the Emperor, Tokoyo would go swimming with the ama – women who dived deep under the sea to find pearl oysters, sea snails and other beautiful shells.

One day the Emperor suddenly fell ill, and Tokoyo's father was called upon to visit him in the palace. The samurai tried to comfort the Emperor, but he could see that the royal leader was no longer himself – his mysterious illness had made him very weak and confused.

Losing his senses, the Emperor turned against Tokoyo's father and banished him to the faraway islands of Oki. The samurai had no time to say goodbye to Tokoyo, who was left behind.

For days, Tokoyo roamed around her empty house, crying for her lost father. The islands of Oki were so far away, and she didn't know if he would ever return.

Although she was still very sad, one day Tokoyo stopped crying. "This will get me nowhere," she said to herself. She dried her tears and decided that the only thing to do was go and find Oribe Shime. "My father is a loyal samurai warrior. I will show the Emperor he has made a mistake."

So Tokoyo sold all their possessions and, taking only her dagger and some food, set off across the countryside of Japan towards the islands of Oki.

After many weeks she finally came to the edge of the Western Sea. She could see the islands in the far distance, but the local fishermen wouldn't ferry her across the water. "It is forbidden to visit the islands of the banished," they told her. "And, in any case, the seas are haunted. We dare not take you over in our boats."

Tokoyo was disappointed but, like a samurai, she was brave and determined, and wouldn't give up easily. *I will have to go alone,* she thought.

That night Tokoyo found an old rowing boat and, under cover of the silky darkness, began to row herself across the water to the nearest island.

When she was about halfway across she sensed a strange silence. She looked around and thought she saw ghosts floating above the water – they were the spirits of people once banished to the islands.

"Turn back now," they whispered in warning.

Although Tokoyo was frightened, she shut her eyes tight and kept on rowing. As the dawning sun began to creep up into the sky, turning the water from inky black to gold, she finally made it to the shore of the nearest island, and the ghosts dissolved in the light of day. She hauled her boat up on to the sand and began her search of the island.

Tokoyo wandered across the island for many days, but no one could tell her where her father was. Finally, exhausted after her long and fruitless search, she sat down under a tree at the top of a cliff, and buried her head in her hands.

As Tokoyo sat there, unsure what to do next, she heard someone crying. Shielding her eyes from the late evening sun, she saw a young girl in a white dress being dragged to the edge of the cliff by a priest.

"No! Stop! What are you doing?" Tokoyo cried, running over and grabbing the priest's arm to stop him.

"You must be a stranger here if you do not know of the terrible curse on these islands," the priest replied. "An evil sea serpent lives here in a cave beneath the ocean. The serpent will whip up terrible storms and destroy us all if we don't sacrifice a young girl to it every year."

Beyond the cliff, the deep sea was crashing against the shore. Tokoyo remembered the samurai code of courage her father had taught her.

"I will go to the sea serpent instead," she said.

Tokoyo put on the girl's white dress and clenched the blade of her dagger between her teeth. Then, taking a deep breath, she dived into the foaming water below.

Tokoyo was rewarded now for all the time she had spent swimming with the ama women. After a few strong kicks she found herself at the bottom of the sea by the serpent's cave.

Outside the cave she saw a small statue of the Emperor. She picked it up and tucked it into her belt, thinking she could use it as another weapon. As she did so, the serpent swam out of its cave and, seeing Tokoyo, lunged towards her.

But Tokoyo was too quick. She twisted out of the serpent's way, landing a blow with her dagger right in its eye as it thundered past. She powered back to the surface for another gulp of air, then dived down again.

The half-blind monster was no match for the brave and determined samurai girl, and Tokoyo quickly outwitted it, striking a fatal blow deep into its evil heart. She then swam back to the shore, dragging the dead beast behind her.

The priest and the young girl couldn't believe their eyes.

"No one has ever fought the sea serpent before," the priest said. "You have saved us all!"

Tokoyo returned to their village, and everyone came out to celebrate. But, even though she was proud of what she had done, Tokoyo did not smile.

"Why are you sad?" asked the young girl.

"My father, Oribe Shime, has been banished to these islands but I cannot find him anywhere," Tokoyo explained.

The young girl's eyes widened, and she ran over to the priest and whispered in his ear.

The priest led Tokoyo to one of the huts in the village, and there she found her father. He hugged her tightly, crying with joy, and incredibly proud of his courageous daughter.

After a few days Tokoyo and her father left the islands of
Oki and began their long journey home.

When they returned, they discovered that the Emperor had
recovered from his strange illness. So they went to the palace,
hoping that he would remember his brave samurai warrior.

"What is that?" asked the Emperor when he saw them,
pointing to the statue in Tokoyo's hand.

Tokoyo told him how she had defeated the sea serpent
and taken the statue of the Emperor from outside its cave.

All the Emperor's advisors started talking excitedly. They
had heard that a strange curse on a figure of the Emperor
was what had caused him to lose his senses. When Tokoyo
killed the sea serpent and took the statue, the curse must
have been broken.

Upon learning what had happened, the Emperor said
Oribe Shime could return to the palace immediately. He
rewarded Tokoyo by allowing her to serve as a samurai
alongside her beloved father. She spent many more happy
days swimming deep in the ocean – but luckily she never
saw another sea serpent!

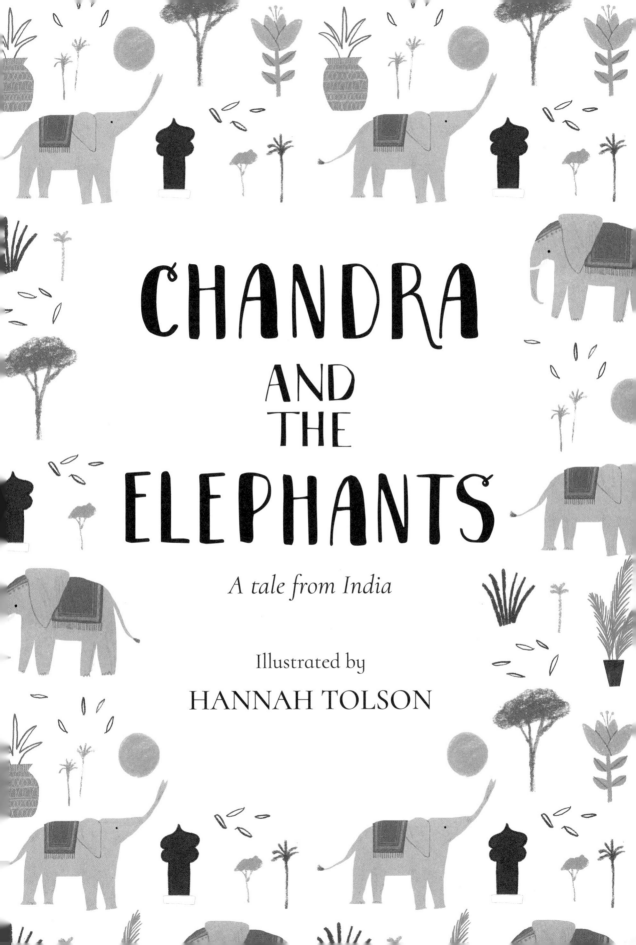

CHANDRA
AND
THE
ELEPHANTS

A tale from India

Illustrated by

HANNAH TOLSON

Chandra lived in India with her parents, who were very hard-working rice farmers. Although her family didn't have a lot of money, Chandra was happy. She especially enjoyed watching the huge elephants that roamed around the village.

"Our ruler, the Rajah, owns those elephants. He is very wise, Chandra," said her father. "He says we farmers must give him all the rice we harvest so he can keep it safe. Then, if there is ever a famine, he will give it back to us so that we don't starve."

"That is very wise indeed," said Chandra's mother.

And so, every harvest, the villagers kept just enough rice for themselves and their families, and gave the rest to the Rajah to store away.

Since there was no extra rice to sell, Chandra helped her parents by getting a job washing the Rajah's elephants. Chandra loved the elephants, and got to know their ways very well.

Then, one year, there was a terrible drought, and the rice harvest failed. The people went to ask the wise Rajah for their rice, but he refused them.

"I am the Rajah," he said. "I must keep all the rice for myself."

Chandra and the villagers were very upset. How would they survive the drought if they had nothing to eat?

One day, as Chandra approached the elephants' stables to give them their daily wash, two big guards stopped her.

"You can't go in there," said one guard. "Rajah's orders."

"Why not?" asked Chandra. "I am the elephants' bather – that's my job."

"That may be," said the second guard. "But the elephants are sick, and the Rajah doesn't want anyone but the elephant doctors with them until they are better."

Saddened, Chandra went home. But she was very worried about the elephants, so every day she went back, and every day she was told the same thing.

Finally, on the fourth day, she could see that the guards were worried.

"What's wrong?" she asked.

"The doctors aren't helping," the first guard told her. "The elephants aren't getting any better."

"Let me see the Rajah," said Chandra. "I know the elephants better than anyone. Maybe I can help."

Reluctantly, the guards took Chandra to see their ruler.

Chandra had never been inside the Rajah's palace before. She gazed open-mouthed at the colourful silk cushions, the beautiful mosaics on the walls and the gorgeous patterned carpets.

The Rajah was sitting under a sunshade, with a chequerboard in front of him, playing a game with one of his advisors.

"Who are you and what do you want?" the Rajah demanded, when the guards brought young Chandra before him.

"Please, Your Excellency," said Chandra. "I am Chandra, and I wash your elephants. Would you let me look at them and see if I can find out what is wrong?"

The Rajah stared down at Chandra. "But you are just a child!" He laughed. "Take her away," he commanded.

"Wait!" said Chandra. "I visit the elephants every day, and I know them very well. Please let me see them."

The Rajah considered the girl. "I prize my elephants above all things," he said at last. "You may see them, and if you can cure them I will give you anything you want."

Chandra was taken immediately to her beloved elephants. She was very shocked to see how sick they were. The elephants crowded round her and stroked her sadly with their trunks.

"You poor things," said Chandra, kissing each one in turn.

She examined every elephant very carefully and, when she looked in their ears, she realized what the problem was. The elephants' ears were blocked. So she got plenty of rags and warm water, and thoroughly cleaned each animal's ears. Sure enough, within a few days the elephants were completely well again.

The Rajah was overjoyed and summoned Chandra to him.

"You have made my elephants better!" he cried. "Tell me what you would like as a reward. Jewels? Fine silks? Name it and it shall be yours."

Chandra thought long and hard. She looked around at the riches of the palace and at the Rajah's splendid clothes. She thought about all the villagers, starving because of the drought, and of the Rajah's storehouses, packed full of rice.

"Some grains of rice, Your Excellency," she said.

"Very well," agreed the Rajah, surprised. "How many do you want?"

Chandra looked at the Rajah's chequerboard. "All I ask is that you place one grain of rice on the first square of your board," she said. "Then two on the second, four on the third, and so on, doubling the amount with each square until you come to the last square."

"Do as she says!" The Rajah clapped his hands, delighted she had asked for so little.

The Rajah's servants began to place rice grains as Chandra had directed. The board had eight rows of eight squares – sixty-four squares in total. The servants doubled the grains on each square, and by the time they reached the first square of the second row, they had to count out 256 grains of rice.

"That's about a spoonful of rice," said Chandra. "To make it easier, why don't you start measuring it in spoonfuls now?"

The servants thought that was a good idea, so they measured two spoonfuls for the next square, and four for the next.

At the end of the second row, Chandra said, "That's about a bowlful of rice. Why don't you start measuring it in bowlfuls now?"

By the end of the third row, the rice filled a large cart. And, by the end of the fifth row, Chandra had emptied the Rajah's entire store!

The Rajah looked on in dismay. "I have no more rice left!" he wailed. "How much rice do I need to finish the board?"

Chandra smiled. "If you keep doubling it up until the last square, the whole country will be knee-deep in rice," she said.

"I cannot give you that much!" the Rajah cried. "What can I do to be released from this promise I can't keep?"

"You must give the rice back to the villagers," said Chandra firmly. "And only keep enough for yourself and your household."

The Rajah agreed. He gave back almost all the rice, and promised never to be so greedy again.

When Chandra returned to the village, her parents were very proud of their clever daughter.

After that, the Rajah was a much wiser ruler; he never again took more rice than he needed. The villagers were able to sell their extra rice so they weren't so poor, but each year they kept a little bit in case there was another famine.

Chandra continued to look after the elephants, and they all loved her even more. And she never looked at a chequerboard again without smiling to herself.

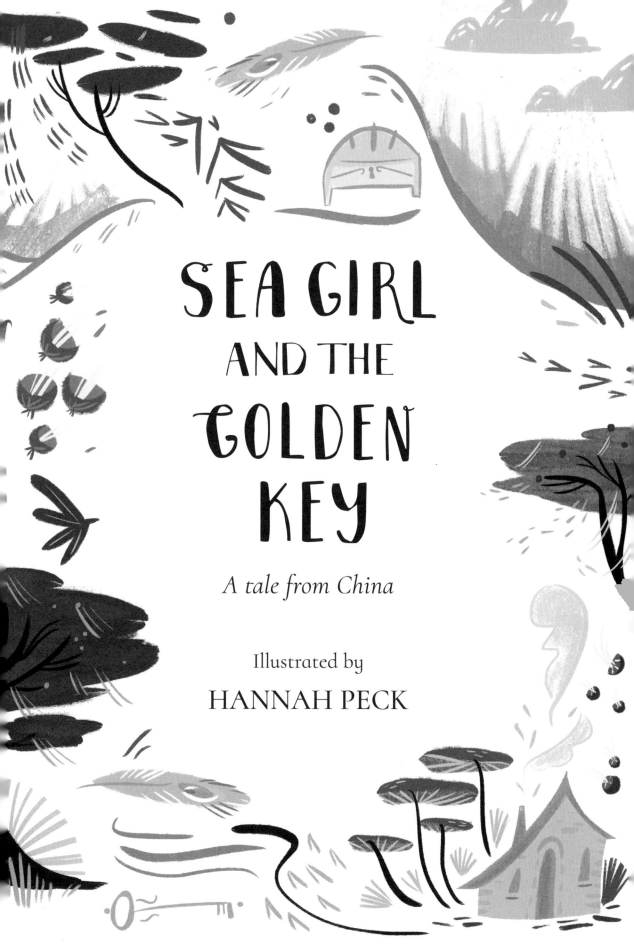

SEA GIRL
AND THE
GOLDEN KEY

A tale from China

Illustrated by

HANNAH PECK

Many years ago, in the far south of China, a terrible drought came to a small village nestled at the foot of a high mountain. There had been no rain for many weeks, the crops were dying in the fields, and the villagers feared they would starve when winter came. One of the farmers had a young daughter named Sea Girl. To help her family, Sea Girl sold brooms made from the wild bamboo that grew on the mountain.

One day Sea Girl was exploring a part of the mountain she had never been to before. She found a thick stand of bamboo that was perfect for making her brooms. Delighted, she started cutting her way through the bamboo with her axe. But, as she did so, she caught a glimpse of blue. She peered through the fronds and saw the most beautiful lake before her. Its waters were smooth and still, reflecting the white clouds floating across the sky above. As she gazed at the lake, she saw a leaf fall from an overhanging willow. Then, from nowhere, a wild goose swooped down and caught the leaf in its beak.

Sea Girl found her way back down the mountain, enchanted by what she had seen.

When Sea Girl climbed the mountain the next day, she was still thinking about the lake. If she could cut a channel from it to create a stream, it would flow down the mountain and water the village's dying crops.

Excited by her idea, she began to look for a likely place. But all around the lake was either thick forest or steep rock. Nowhere seemed suitable. She was about to give up, when she came across a high stone wall. It was half hidden by leaves and covered in dark green moss, and Sea Girl knew that the lake water must be on the other side of it. She pushed as hard as she could against it, even using her axe to try and break it down, but it was no use. Exhausted and disheartened, she slumped to the ground. As she did so, the wild goose she had seen the day before glided down from the sky and landed beside her.

"If you want to open this stone gate, Sea Girl," it said, "you will need the golden key."

It pointed with its wing and, sure enough, there was a tiny keyhole in the gate that Sea Girl hadn't noticed before.

Sea Girl was so surprised to hear a goose speaking that she forgot to ask where the key was. But, as quickly as it had arrived, the goose flapped away.

Sea Girl scrambled to her feet. Where to start looking for the key? She searched around the gate, but found nothing, so she set off along the lakeshore in hope of inspiration. After a while she stopped to rest under a large cypress tree. Perched on a low branch above her head was a parrot with bright red and green feathers. The bird cocked its head to look at her.

"Do you know where the key is, parrot?" she asked out loud, smiling to herself.

"The Dragon King guards the lake," said the parrot. "He has the golden key."

By now, Sea Girl was so tired that a talking parrot did not take her by surprise. "So, how do I find him?" she asked.

"You must summon his third daughter," said the parrot. "She is very lonely in the palace, and she will help you." And, with that, it flew off into the forest.

"That may be true," Sea Girl muttered, "but how do I summon the Dragon King's third daughter?"

"You must sing to her," said a voice from behind her. Sea Girl swung round, and there stood a magnificent peacock, its tail spread in a dazzling fan of shining gold, green and blue.

"Sing?" asked Sea Girl.

"That's right. Sing her the songs of your people, and she'll come to you from the lake." Then the peacock swept away, leaving a gleaming feather at Sea Girl's feet.

Sea Girl picked up the feather, cleared her throat and began to sing. Her strong voice carried across the still waters of the lake. As the last echo of her song faded away, she waited hopefully, but the Dragon King's daughter did not come. So Sea Girl sang a different song, this time about the wind whistling through the bamboo. Still nothing. Then she sang of cherry blossom, white as snow.

Suddenly a girl magically burst from the lake's shallows in a shower of crystal droplets.

"How fascinating your songs are," she said. "I tried to resist them – my father does not allow us to meet mortals – but in the end I had to come."

"Are you the Dragon King's third daughter?" asked Sea Girl.

"Yes, I am Third Daughter," the girl replied. "But who are you? Why are you singing here?"

"I'm from the village at the foot of the mountain," said Sea Girl. "We need water from this lake to save our crops, so I've come to ask you for the golden key that opens the stone gate."

Third Daughter thought for a moment. "My father keeps the key in his treasure cave, which is guarded by a giant eagle," she said, her eyes sparkling with mischief. "But, if you wait here until my father goes away, I'll come and help you."

Sea Girl waited patiently for three days and three nights.

Finally, Third Daughter returned.

"My father has gone," she said. "But we must be quick."

She led Sea Girl to the Dragon King's treasure cave and, sure enough, perched high on the rocks above the cave's entrance was a giant eagle.

"We should sing to the eagle to distract it," whispered Sea Girl, as they hid behind some reeds near the cave.

So Sea Girl and Third Daughter took it in turns to sing the most interesting songs they knew. Curious, the eagle flew down to investigate. Third Daughter crept away through the reeds, still singing, and the eagle followed her captivating voice.

Sea Girl stole into the cave and was dazzled by the glittering jewels and gold inside. But she ignored all the treasure and began searching for the key. It seemed an impossible task – but then she saw a small wooden box, plain and dull against all the shining gems.

Could it possibly in there? she thought. Holding her breath, she opened the box. A tiny golden key lay inside.

Sea Girl ran out of the cave to Third Daughter, who immediately stopped singing. Losing interest, the eagle flew back to its lookout and the two girls hurried back to the stone gate.

They put the key into the lock and turned it.

The gate ground open and water gushed from the lake down the mountainside to the village. It filled the pools and channels around the fields, while the villagers looked on in delight. Thanks to Sea Girl, they would never go hungry again.

But now the water was coming too fast!

"Quickly!" cried Third Daughter. "We must close the gate or the village will be flooded!" The girls put all their weight against the gate, but the water was too strong. They couldn't move the gate so much as an inch.

Sea Girl cut down some bamboo to try to stem the flow, but it wasn't enough.

"I have an idea," said Sea Girl. She started to pile rocks into the gap. Third Daughter began to help her, rolling boulders across the gateway, when something magical happened. The bamboo that Sea Girl had put there turned to stone and the flow subsided to a gentle stream.

The girls were exhausted but happy. The village was saved, thanks to a lot of hard work – and a touch of magic!

A few days later, the Dragon King returned and saw what Third Daughter had done. He flew into a terrible rage and banished her from the palace below the lake.

Third Daughter came down the mountain to the village, where the villagers welcomed her with open arms and promised that she would never be lonely again. She and Sea Girl sang happily together every day, making up funny songs about talking parrots and hidden treasure.

THE
SNOW
QUEEN

A tale from Hans Christian Andersen

Illustrated by

HOLLY HATAM

In a time long ago, when even the animals talked, there was a particularly wicked hobgoblin who liked nothing better than to make mischief and trouble. One day the hobgoblin put a curse on a mirror so that everything it reflected would look rotten and ugly. She was so delighted with her mirror that she travelled around the world with it, showing other demons, trolls and goblins how it made even the loveliest landscape look like boiled spinach, turned the most handsome man ugly, and ruined magnificent cities.

"This is wonderful," said one demon, cackling wildly. "Let's take it up to the heavens and see how ugly the angels look in it."

So the hobgoblin and the demons and the trolls and the other goblins flew up into the skies, screeching with laughter. Even the mirror was laughing, and it shook so much that it slipped out of the hobgoblin's grasp and fell back down to earth. There it shattered into thousands of pieces – some as large as windowpanes, and some so small they could barely be seen. A few of the smallest splinters found their way into people's hearts and eyes, making it so that they felt nothing but misery and saw nothing but ugliness.

Many years later, a girl and a boy called Gerda and Kai lived next door to each other in two tall houses in the city. Their bedrooms were in the attic of each house, and their windows opened on to the roof, where the two children would often play.

Gerda's grandmother had planted beautiful roses in pots on the roof, so it felt like they were in a garden. The children liked nothing better than to sit up there and listen to the old lady tell them stories, especially the one about the mysterious Snow Queen who ruled over the dancing snowflakes.

Kai was convinced he had seen her once, peering at him through the frosted glass of his window before flying away into the night on her sleigh in a thick flurry of snowflakes.

One day Gerda and Kai were playing, when Kai suddenly squeezed his eyes shut. He felt a sharp pain in his eye and a cold tingle in his heart. He didn't know it, but he had got splinters of the hobgoblin's evil mirror in his eye and a shard of it in his heart. When he opened his eyes again, everything looked horrid, and he felt hatred and anger boiling inside him.

"I don't want to play with you any more," he said cruelly to Gerda. "I don't even like you, or your boring grandmother."

Gerda was confused and hurt by what her friend had said, but she chose to leave him alone, as he had asked.

One morning the next winter, Kai was playing alone in the snow. He decided to go to the town square and fasten his sledge to one of the bigger sleighs, like the other boys did, to hitch a free ride. Just then, a magnificent white sleigh sped past him and he caught hold of it. But the sleigh didn't stop when it reached the square – it carried on through the city and out into the countryside.

The snow was falling more and more thickly, and Kai was beginning to feel frightened, when suddenly the sleigh stopped and its driver called to him.

Kai squinted through the swirling snow and gasped when he saw who it was. The Snow Queen herself! She was dressed in white furs, and when she moved, Kai heard the tinkling of icicles. The queen was enchanting, and Kai found he could not resist her when she summoned him.

He climbed in beside her and she wrapped him in furs, which felt like being buried in soft snow. She gave him a cold kiss on his forehead, casting a spell, and Kai instantly forgot all about Gerda and his home.

Laughing, the Snow Queen flicked the reins and the sleigh sped away.

Back in the city, Gerda was worried when Kai didn't come home. Even though Kai had treated her coldly, he was still her friend, so she went to look for him by the river.

"Kai!" she called, but there was no reply.

Gerda climbed into a boat and floated down the river to a cottage with a beautiful rose garden – which was strange, as it was still winter outside.

As she approached, a lady came out of the cottage.

"Have you seen a little boy come past here?" called Gerda. "He loves roses like the ones you have here."

"I'm afraid I haven't," said the woman, smiling. "Why don't you come inside and have some cherries?"

Gerda followed the kind lady into the cottage. However, as she ate the cherries, her memory of Kai faded away. The lady was actually a witch! Using her powers, the witch made Gerda want nothing more than to stay with her. She also made her roses sink back into the ground so they wouldn't remind Gerda of her friend.

For a while Gerda lived happily with the lady. Then, one day, the witch put on a hat painted with roses, and when Gerda saw it her memories of Kai flooded back.

"I must go and find my friend!" she cried, and ran out of the cottage.

Gerda ran until she could run no longer. She stopped, exhausted, under a tree in which a crow was perched. The crow hopped down and looked at her with its head on one side.

"I don't suppose you have seen my friend Kai, have you?" Gerda asked the crow wearily. "He is my age, with brown hair and dark eyes."

"I do know of a boy who looks like that," said the crow. "He has just married a princess here. Would you like me to take you to him?"

"Oh, yes please," said Gerda.

So the crow took Gerda to a palace nearby, and sneaked her inside to meet the princess and her new prince – but the prince was not Kai.

Gerda told the prince and princess her story, and they were so touched they gave her a carriage and horses to continue her search. Grateful, Gerda set off again on her adventure, across the fields and into a dark forest.

As the carriage made its way through the trees, Gerda heard shouting outside. In a flash, a band of robbers surrounded her carriage and horses. They were about to drag Gerda – who was kicking and yelling – out of the carriage when a voice suddenly cried, "Stop!"

It was the daughter of one of the robbers. "I want her as a playmate!" the girl demanded.

The robbers took Gerda back with them to their lair. Gerda played with the Robber Girl and her pet reindeer, Bae. As they were settling down to sleep, Gerda told the Robber Girl about Kai.

Some pigeons roosting in the rafters overheard, and the next day they flew down to speak to the girls.

"We know where Kai is," they cooed. "The Snow Queen put him under her spell and carried him away to Lapland!"

"Bae can take you there!" the Robber Girl said to Gerda. She gave Gerda some boots and food, and sent her off on the reindeer's back.

Along the way, Gerda and Bae met friendly people and animals who gave them shelter and food to eat. One wise lady knew where the Snow Queen lived.

"Gerda, you have a special power," she said kindly. "You can save Kai with the magic of love."

So Gerda and Bae continued their journey to the Snow Queen's palace in Lapland. When they drew close, Bae let Gerda down from her back. "You are a brave and loyal girl, Gerda," she said. "You must make your own way from this point. I will wait for you here."

Gerda saw the icy palace up ahead and began to plough through the thick snow. Hundreds of snowflakes swarmed around her, stinging her cold face like icy wasps, as though trying to stop her. But her breath turned into angel snowflakes and beat back the wicked snow.

At last Gerda reached the palace. She ran through dozens of empty frozen rooms, calling for Kai. Finally, she found him in a vast chamber, sitting on the steps of a frozen throne, playing with the pieces of an ice puzzle.

"Gerda! You found me!" he said. "The Snow Queen kidnapped me, and now I cannot leave until I make these pieces of ice into a word."

Gerda hugged his freezing body to hers, crying with relief. Her warm, loving tears melted the shard of evil glass in his heart, and he began to cry too, washing the specks of mirror out of his eye.

When the children looked down, the pieces of puzzle were dancing around, and then arranging themselves into the word *ETERNITY*.

"Come on!" said Gerda. "You're free!"

They hurried out of the palace and back to Bae. Then, with the help of all Gerda's friends, they made their way back home.

"You're alive!" said Gerda's grandmother, overjoyed to see them. "My, how you've grown!"

Gerda and Kai looked at each other, astonished. For, sure enough, they were all grown up. The two friends were so happy, and they rushed up to the rooftop to see the beautiful roses that still bloomed there.

ETERNITY

"I'M NOT AFRAID

FOR I'M

OF STORMS, LEARNING HOW TO SAIL MY SHIP"

– Louisa May Alcott

LADYBIRD BOOKS

UK | USA | Canada | Ireland | Australia
India | New Zealand | South Africa

Ladybird Books is part of the Penguin Random House group of companies
whose addresses can be found at global.penguinrandomhouse.com

www.penguin.co.uk   www.puffin.co.uk   www.ladybird.co.uk

First published by Ladybird Books Ltd, 2018
001

Introduction copyright © Jacqueline Wilson, 2018
Stories retold by Julia Bruce
"Gretel and Hansel" illustrated by Olga Baumert
"Tamasha and the Troll" illustrated by Molley May
"Tokoyo and the Sea Serpent" illustrated by Kerry Hyndman
"Chandra and the Elephants" illustrated by Hannah Tolson
"Sea Girl and the Golden Key" illustrated by Hannah Peck
"The Snow Queen" illustrated by Holly Hatam
Copyright © Ladybird Books Ltd, 2018

Printed in Italy

A CIP catalogue record for this book is available from the British Library

ISBN: 978–0–241–35589–3

All correspondence to:
Ladybird Books
Penguin Random House Children's
80 Strand, London WC2R 0RL